Walt Disney's Peter Pan

Adapted from the film by Todd Strasser

New York

Library of Congress Catalog Card Number: 93-72170
ISBN: 1-56282-640-9

Walt Disney's

Peter Pan

1

ate one dark, cloudy evening a long time
ago, in a three-story brick house on a
quiet cobblestoned street in London,
George Darling and his wife, Mary, were
preparing to go to a party. Mary was wearing
a white-and-lavender evening gown and was
seated at her dressing table, pulling a brush
through her light brown hair. George, a tall,
dark-haired man with a prominent belly and
gruff voice, was searching for something in
his dresser.

"George, dear," said Mary. "Do hurry. We
mustn't be late for the party."

"Unless I find my cuff links," George
grumbled, "we don't go to the party." He
pulled open one drawer after another. "And if
we don't go to the party, I can never show my
face in the office again."

Having worked his way down to the
lowest drawer in the dresser, George abruptly
straightened up and promptly banged his head
into the bottom of the highest drawer.

"*Yeow!*" he cried. The evening was not getting off to a good start.

Upstairs in the children's nursery, the Darlings' two young sons were hopping from bed to bed, dueling playfully with wooden swords.

"Take that!" shouted Michael, a tow-headed boy of four, as he swung his sword from his perch on the bed.

"Blast you, Peter Pan!" his older brother, John, shouted back. John was eight and wore glasses and a pirate's red bandanna. Both boys were dressed for bed.

"Give up, Captain Hook?" demanded Michael triumphantly as he pinned back his brother's sword.

"Never!" yelled John. He picked up a wooden clothes hanger in his right hand and brandished it as a hook. "I'll teach you to cut off my hand." He caught Michael's ankle with the hanger, causing him to tumble onto the bed.

At that moment Wendy, the eldest of the Darling children, came into the nursery. She was a pretty girl of twelve, with her mother's light brown hair and large blue eyes.

"No, John," she corrected. "It was the *left* hand."

"Oh," said John, acknowledging his mistake. "Thank you, Wendy." John placed the hanger in his left hand and promptly resumed the duel. Just then Nana, the family's Saint Bernard, trotted into the room with a tray on her head. On the tray was a bottle of codfish oil, three glasses of water, and three spoons. Besides being a dog, Nana was also the children's nursemaid.

"Oh, Nana," said Wendy, wrinkling her nose. "Must we take that nasty codfish oil every night?"

Nana set the tray on a table and went about straightening the room.

"Scuttle me bones, boy!" shouted John as he chased Michael around the bed. "I'll slit your gizzard!"

"Oh no you won't!" countered Michael. "Back, you villain!"

"Insolent pup!" John yelled, and lunged toward Michael.

Nana instantly pricked up her ears. *Such language*, her astonished look seemed to suggest. Meanwhile, the duel raged on. The boys fought valiantly. Then Michael caught John off guard, and his wooden sword found its mark. John gasped and clutched his chest, pretending to be mortally wounded. Just then the nursery door swung open, and in strode their father with his collar unbuttoned and his shirt open.

"Boys, boys, less noise. Please!" Still in search of his missing cuff links, George began rummaging through a dresser.

"Hello, Father," said John pleasantly from the middle of his death scene.

"You old bilge rat!" cried Michael, brandishing his sword at his brother.

George spun around. "Now see here, Michael!"

"Not *you*, Father," said John, pointing at Michael. "You see, *he's* Peter Pan."

"And John's Captain Hook," explained Michael.

"Yes, yes, of course," replied their father impatiently. "Have either of you seen my gold cuff links?"

Guiltily John leaned close to Michael and whispered, "The buried treasure—where is it?"

Michael shook his head. "I don't know."

"Then where's the treasure map?" John asked nervously.

"It got lost," said Michael.

From under John's bedding George found at least one thing he'd been looking for. "Thank heavens," he grumbled. "My shirt front!" He started to put it on, oblivious to the brightly colored treasure map drawn on it.

"You found it!" cried Michael as he grabbed for the map.

"Don't paw at me, Michael," said his father firmly. George gently pried his son's fingers from his shirt front. "This is my last clean—" Suddenly the shirt front flipped up, and he noticed for the first time the markings all over it.

"Oh no!" shouted George.

Mary entered the nursery looking for her husband. "George, dear," she prompted, "we really must hurry or we'll be late."

"But look!" said her husband irritably. He pointed at the treasure map.

"It's only chalk, Father," Michael explained.

Mary frowned sternly and put her hands on her hips. "Why, Michael!"

"It's not his fault," said John, coming to his younger brother's defense. "It's in the story. Wendy said—"

"Wendy?" her father bellowed. "Story? I

might have known." He stormed over to the doorway. "Wendy!" he shouted.

"Yes, Father?" answered Wendy breezily. She came into the nursery carrying a bowl and a pitcher, which she set on the soap stand. Before her father could begin to scold her, Wendy noticed her mother's gown and beamed. "Oh, Mother!" cried Wendy. "You look simply lovely!"

"Thank you, dear," said Mary, smiling. She affected a tone of nonchalance, but it was obvious she was pleased. "It's just my old gown done over, but it did turn out rather nicely."

"Mary . . . ," George interrupted. "If you don't mind."

Wendy turned to her father, and her eyes went wide with alarm. "Why, Father!" Wendy gasped. "What have you done to your shirt?"

"What have *I* done?" said her father incredulously.

"Really, George, it comes right off," said Mary as she scrubbed off the chalk marks with a handkerchief.

"That's no excuse," he said angrily. He turned to address his daughter. "Wendy, haven't I warned you about stuffing the boys' heads with a lot of silly stories?"

"But they're not silly stories," protested Wendy.

"I say they are," insisted her father. "Captain Crook and Peter Pirate!"

"Peter *Pan*, Father," corrected Wendy.

"Peter Poppycock!" shouted George in frustration.

"Oh, no, Father," said Wendy.

"You don't understand," said John.

"I understand perfectly!" George turned to his wife. "Mary," he said resolutely, "this child's growing up. It's high time she had a room of her own!"

Mary was stunned. Wendy, too. She stared at her father in shocked disbelief.

"No!" cried Michael finally.

"Yes," said George firmly. He turned to Wendy. "This is your last night in the nursery, young lady. And that's my final word on the matter."

George turned, promptly tripped over Nana, and smacked into the dresser, sending everything on it crashing to the floor. "Poor Nana!" cried Mary and the children as they rushed past to see if Nana was all right.

George was dumbfounded.

"*Poor Nana?*" cried George in disbelief. "That's the last straw!" George jumped to his feet and grabbed Nana by the collar. "And there'll be no more dogs for nursemaids in this house, either!"

The children cried and protested desperately, but it was no use. When their father was angry, he never listened to reason. They waved a sad farewell as George dragged Nana from the nursery.

"Dash it all, Nana," George complained. "Don't look at me like that. It's nothing personal." George felt miserable as he tied Nana to a post in the backyard. "It's just that you're not really a nurse at all. You're a dog. And the children aren't puppies, they're people. And sooner or later, people have to grow up."

Upstairs in the nursery, Mary tucked the boys into bed and sat at her daughter's bedside.

"But I don't want to grow up," Wendy insisted sadly.

"Now dear," said her mother gently as she pulled up the covers and kissed her daughter on the forehead. "Don't worry anymore about it tonight."

"He called Peter Pan absolute poppycock," John said.

Mary set her son's glasses and pirate bandanna on the nightstand. "I'm sure he didn't mean it. Your father was just upset."

"Poor Nana," sniffed Michael. "Out there all alone."

"No more tears, Michael," said his mother softly. "It's a warm night. She'll be all right."

Mary went to the window and started to close it.

"Please don't lock it," Wendy called out from her bed. "He might come back."

"He?" asked her mother.

"Peter Pan," Wendy said. "You see, I found something that belongs to him."

"And what's that?" Mary asked.

"His shadow." Wendy yawned, and her eyes grew heavy with sleep. "Nana had it, but I took it away."

"Yes, of course." Her mother smiled. "Now, good night, dear." She turned off the light and slipped quietly out.

A few minutes later Mary and George Darling were on their way to the party. George wore a top hat and carried a cane. His wife wore a cape.

"Do you think the children will be safe without Nana?" Mary asked.

"Why wouldn't they be?" George replied.

"Well, Wendy said something about a shadow."

"Shadow?" her husband repeated. "Whose shadow?"

"Peter Pan's," said Mary.

"Peter Pan's?" George frowned. "Oh, Mary, of all the childish fiddle-faddle."

"There must've been someone," his wife insisted.

George threw up his hands in exasperation. "How can we expect the children to grow up and be practical when you're as bad as they are?" he complained angrily. "No wonder Wendy has these wild ideas."

Of course her husband was right, Mary Darling thought. All this talk of shadows and Peter Pan was just what her husband said it was: fiddle-faddle. Just childish nonsense.

Mary sighed as she took her husband's arm. It is a pity, though, she admitted.

She had rather liked the idea of Peter Pan.

2

No sooner had George and Mary Darling turned the corner than Peter Pan flew out of the sky and alighted on the gabled roof of the Darling home. He was followed by a small, shimmering pixie named Tinker Bell. Peter wore forest green clothes and a green cap with an orange feather. He waited until the Darlings were out of sight, then made sure Nana was asleep in the yard before he jumped down to the nursery window. All three children were asleep in their beds, so Peter and Tinker Bell slipped inside.

Peter pointed to the doghouse. "Look in there, Tink."

Tinker Bell flew into the doghouse, then came out and shook her head.

"Darn." Peter glanced around the room. "It must be here somewhere." His eyes settled on the toy chest, and he flew over to have a look. Meanwhile, Tinker Bell found a pretty music box and opened it. Lovely music floated into the air.

"Stop playing," said Peter a bit harshly. "Help me find my shadow."

Stung by Peter's tone, Tinker Bell ignored him and flew off to admire herself in a mirror. She heard a rattling sound coming from a nearby drawer and peeked through the keyhole. The shadow was inside. Tinker Bell jingled for Peter's attention.

Peter rushed over and yanked open the drawer. The shadow leapt out. "Come back here!" Peter cried. He slammed the drawer shut, accidentally trapping Tinker Bell inside. The shadow dashed up the wall. Peter flew after it.

His shadow scooted across the ceiling and down the far wall, where it tried to hide behind a chair. Peter dove after it, knocking over the soap stand and waking Wendy.

She sat up in bed and rubbed her eyes. "Peter Pan!" she gasped.

Wendy hopped out of bed and ran to Peter. "I knew you'd come back!" she jabbered excitely. "I saved your shadow for you. I do hope it isn't rumpled."

Peter backed into the corner. He wanted to escape, but he couldn't until his shadow was firmly reattached. He grabbed the soap from the stand and rubbed it on his feet, hoping to get his shadow to stick.

"You know, you look exactly the way I thought you would," Wendy ran on breathlessly. Then she realized what he was trying to do and took the soap away. "No, silly, you can't stick it on with soap. It needs sewing." She marched across the room to her dresser and took out her sewing kit. "Of course, I knew it was your shadow the minute I saw it, and I said to myself, I'll put it away for him until he comes back." She smiled at Peter. "I knew you'd come back. After all, one can't leave his shadow lying about and not miss it sooner or later."

Peter scratched his head. He'd never heard anyone rattle on so.

Wendy opened her sewing kit and started to thread a needle. "What I still don't understand is how Nana got your shadow in the first place. She really isn't vicious, you know. And she's a wonderful nurse, although Father says—"

"Girls talk too much," Peter blurted out.

Embarrassed, Wendy put down the needle. "Well, yes, I do sometimes."

"But don't stop sewing, girl," Peter said.

"My name isn't girl," Wendy replied, picking up her needle and commencing to sew. "It's Wendy Moira Angela Dar—"

Peter put up a hand. "Wendy's enough," he said rather rudely.

Wendy, however, was far too curious to be offended by his bad manners. She wanted to know more about Peter. "How did Nana get your shadow?" she asked excitedly.

"She jumped at me the other night," Peter said. "At the window."

"What were you doing there?" Wendy asked as she sewed.

"I came to listen to the stories," Peter said.

"*My* stories?" said Wendy with surprise. "But they're all about *you*."

"Of course," Peter said without a trace of modesty. "That's why I like them. I tell them to the Lost Boys."

Wendy finished sewing and broke off the thread. "Oh, yes, the Lost Boys are your men."

"That's right." Peter hopped off the bed and studied his shadow against the wall. Wendy had sewn it on quite tightly, and it wasn't about to get away again.

"I'm so glad you came back tonight," Wendy said. "I might never have seen you."

"Why?" asked Peter, who was still admiring his shadow.

Wendy turned away and sighed. "Because I have to grow up tomorrow," she said.

Peter spun around, shocked. "Grow up?"

Wendy nodded sadly. "Tonight's my last night in the nursery."

"But that means no more stories," Peter said.

"I know," Wendy said with a sniff.

Peter was incensed. "No, I won't have it!" He grabbed her hand and led her across the room. "Come on!"

Wendy blinked uncomprehendingly. "Where are we going?" she asked.

"Never Land," said Peter. He pulled her to the open window. "You'll never grow up there."

"Oh, Peter, that would be wonderful!" Wendy gasped. But before he could pull her out the window, she stopped. "Wait! What would Mother say?"

"Mother?" Peter said, scowling. "What's a mother?"

Wendy was incredulous. "A mother's someone who loves you and cares for you and tells you stories."

"Good," said Peter, grabbing Wendy by the hand. "You'll be our mother!"

"Now just a minute," said Wendy, backing away from the window. "I have to pack and leave a note where I'll be. Of course, I couldn't stay too long, but . . . " She stopped. I'm being far too practical, she thought. Then she smiled. The idea of going with Peter filled her with the most exquisite joy. "Never Land!" She clasped her hands together. "I'm so happy I think I'll give you a kiss."

Unbeknownst to Wendy and Peter, Tinker Bell had listened to the entire conversation. Still trapped in the dresser drawer, the pixie had grown jealous of Wendy. At the thought of that talkative girl kissing Peter, Tinker Bell doubled her effort to escape. She forced the drawer open and burst into the air.

Across the room, Peter was backing away uncertainly from Wendy. "What's a kiss?" he asked warily.

"I'll show you," Wendy said. She stepped up to him and pursed her lips. Suddenly something yanked her back by the hair!

"Stop it, Tink!" scolded Peter. He chased the pixie around the room.

This time it was Michael who was

awakened. He sat up in his bed, his eyes as wide as saucers. "John! John, wake up!" he shouted. "He's here!"

John sat up groggily, slipped on his glasses, and gasped as he watched Peter catch Tinker Bell in his hat and fly back to Wendy.

"What in the world was that?" Wendy asked, straightening her hair.

"Tinker Bell," Peter said, opening his hat to show her the pixie. "I don't know what's gotten into her."

Michael and John ran over and gazed with wonder into the hat.

"Look," said Michael, "a firefly!"

"A pixie," Wendy said.

Inside Peter's hat, Tinker Bell jingled angrily, creating a tiny shower of sparkles.

"What's the pixie doing?" Michael asked.

"Talking," Peter replied.

"What did she say?" asked Wendy.

Peter laughed. "She says you're a big ugly girl." Tinker Bell huffily flew out of the hat and alighted on a bookcase.

"Well," said Wendy good-naturedly, "I think she's lovely."

Peter pointed to the open window. "Come on, Wendy, let's go."

"Where are we going?" Michael asked.

"To Never Land," Wendy answered excitedly. "Peter's taking us."

"Us?" Peter scowled.

"I couldn't go without Michael and John," Wendy said.

"I should like very much to cross swords with some real buccaneers," John said eagerly.

"And fight pirates, too," Michael added.

Peter smiled. "All right, but you have to take orders," he added sternly.

"Aye, aye, sir!" John said, and saluted sharply.

"Me, too," Michael said with a salute of his own.

"But how do we get to Never Land?" Wendy asked. She'd never seen it on a map, so she imagined it must be very far away indeed.

"We fly," Peter said simply.

"Fly?" Wendy said in a tone both astonished and delighted. "But how?"

"It's easy. All you have to do is . . ." Peter fell silent for a moment and rubbed his chin. "That's funny."

"What's the matter?" asked Wendy. "Don't you know how?"

"Sure," Peter said. "It's just that I never thought about it before." He thought some more. "That's it!" he cried, snapping his fingers. "You have to think of a wonderful thought."

"Any happy little thought?" John and Wendy asked.

"Uh-huh." Peter nodded.

"Like toys at Christmas?" asked Wendy.

"And sleigh bells and snow?" John added.

"Yup. Now watch. Here I go!" And just like that, Peter rose into the air. "Now you try."

"I'll think of a mermaid lagoon underneath a magic moon," said Wendy.

"I'll think I'm in a pirate's cave," said John.

"I'll be an Indian brave!" cried Michael.

Everyone held hands as Peter pulled them up into the air and then let go. Wendy and the boys floated for a moment near the ceiling but suddenly tumbled down and landed with a muffled *thump!* on the bed. Tinker Bell snickered scornfully. Hovering in the air, Peter frowned.

"What's the matter with you?" he asked. "All it takes is a little faith and trust." Then he remembered. "Oh, there's something I forgot. Dust!"

Peter caught Tinker Bell, gave her a vigorous shake, and showered fairy dust over the Darling children like a fine powdery snow.

"Now," Peter instructed them, "think of the happiest things. It's the same as having wings."

"Let's all try it once more," Wendy told the children. Suddenly she and her brothers began to float.

"Look!" John cried. "We're rising off the floor!"

"We can fly!" they cried.

Peter stood on the window ledge and watched them circle the chandelier. "Come on, everybody!" he called. "Here we go—off to Never Land!" Out the window they went, Wendy first; then John in a top hat and carrying an umbrella, just as his father did when he went out; and Michael last, tugging at the arm of his teddy bear. They sailed over the rooftops, past Big Ben, then up through the cloudy sky toward the second star and straight on till morning.

3

The pirate ship with a skull affixed to its bowsprit lay at anchor in the turquoise water near the green island of Never Land. A black flag with a white skull and crossbones flew from atop its mainmast, and from afar one could hear the pirates singing:

> *A pirate's life is a wonderful life*
> *A-rovin' over the sea.*
> *Give me a career as a buccaneer*
> *It's the life of a pirate for me.*
> *Yes, a pirate's life is a wonderful life,*
> *They never bury your bones.*
> *For when it's all over, a jolly sea rover*
> *Drops in on his friend, Davey Jones.*

But the pirates were in a foul mood. They loafed on deck, tossing knives at a crudely rendered picture of the ship's captain drawn on a door. Soon the same door opened and a short, nearsighted mate named Smee trundled out carrying a tray of shaving articles.

"Good morning, shipmates," Smee called out cheerfully.

"What's so good about it, Mr. Smee?" sneered a pirate with a knife clenched between his teeth.

"Yeah," growled a second pirate. "Here we are collecting barnacles on this miserable island while the captain plays ring-around-the-rosy with Peter Pan."

Suddenly Smee found himself staring down the barrel of a loaded musket. The pirate holding the musket grinned as if pulling the trigger would make him the happiest outlaw on the high seas.

"Look out," Smee warned him innocently. "It might go off!"

"We ought to be tending to the business of looting ships," another pirate snarled, stringing Smee up with rope.

A fourth pirate cut the rope with a cutlass and grumbled, "Why, I've almost forgotten how to slit a throat!"

Smee slipped away and clambered quickly onto the poop deck.

"Tell the captain we want to put to sea!" the angry pirates shouted.

Up on the poop deck, Captain Hook sat

at a table, puffing on a cigar and tracing a map of the island with his shining metal hook.

"Blast that Peter Pan," he grumbled, rubbing the dark stubble on his chin. "If I could only find his hideout, I'd trap him in his lair." He studied the map more closely. He and his men had already searched Mermaid Lagoon— *and* Cannibal Cove. Hook contemplated an area on the map marked Indian Camp.

"No, no, no!" he cried in disgust, jumping up from the table. "That's Indian territory." Then he had an idea. Those Indians knew the island better than he knew his ship, he said to himself. Hook sat down again and twirled his mustache. Perhaps he could use them to find Peter Pan's hideout!

His thoughts were interrupted by the arrival of Smee. "Good morning, Captain," said Smee brightly.

"I've got it!" Hook shouted, catching Smee by the shirt and pulling him close. "The answer is Tiger Lily."

"Tiger Lily?" repeated Smee.

"The Indian chief's daughter," explained the captain. His eyes sparkled dark, and an evil grin split his face from ear to ear. "She'll know where Peter Pan is hiding."

Hook released Smee, who backed away. "But will she talk?" asked Smee.

"A little *persuasion* might be in order," the captain replied with a nasty sneer. "Boiling in oil, for instance. Or keelhauling? Marooning?"

Smee nodded agreeably as he mixed shaving lather in a cup. He smiled, knowing that nothing delighted the captain more than the idea of capturing Peter Pan. Hook's cheerful mood was spoiled, however, when a pirate perched up high on a yardarm began singing.

Oh, a pirate's life is a wonderful life,
You'll find adventure and sport.
But live every minute for all that is in it,
For the life of a pirate is short.

If I have to listen to that blasted song one more time! Hook thought. Snarling, he drew his pistol and fired. Smee jumped and shook his head. A moment later he heard a splash.

"Oh dear, Captain," said Smee calmly. "Shooting a man in the middle of his cadenza ain't good form."

Hook turned and glared at Mr. Smee. "*Good form*, Smee?" He leapt to his feet, overturning the table and map. "Blast good form!" he shouted. He backed Smee up against the ship's railing and waved his gleaming hook under the poor man's nose. "Did Pan show good form when he did this to me?"

"Cutting off your hand was only a childish prank," Smee suggested.

"Yes," Hook admitted. "But throwing it to that crocodile!" he fumed. "That cursed beast liked the taste so much, he's followed me ever since, licking his chops for the rest."

The thought of that huge reptile hungering for his flesh took the wind out of Hook. He slumped miserably into his chair and waited for his morning shave.

"And he would've had you by now," said Smee, tucking a sheet under the captain's chin, "if he hadn't swallowed that alarm clock. But now whenever he's near he warns you with that ticktock, ticktock, ticktock."

Still making the ticktock sound, Smee turned to get the shaving articles. The ticktocking grew louder and more distinct. It was coming closer and closer. Suddenly very frightened, Hook peered over the side of the ship's railing. From under the sea the huge green crocodile climbed on a rock and bared his jaws.

Hook leapt from his chair into Smee's arms. "Save me, Smee!" he cried pitifully. "Please don't let him get me! Please!" He pushed Smee to the railing.

"Here now," Smee shouted at the crocodile. "Shame on you for upsetting the poor captain. There'll be no handouts today. Now shoo. Go on, off with ya."

With a sullen look, the crocodile slipped back into the water.

Hook cowered behind his chair. "Is he gone?" he asked Smee in a trembling voice.

"Aye, Captain," Smee replied soothingly. "It's all clear. Nothing to worry about."

"Oh, Smee, Smee," Hook moaned as Smee helped him into his chair. "I can't stand it any longer. I can't!"

"Just relax, Captain," said Smee. He wrapped a warm towel on Hook's face. "What you need is a nice soothing shave."

Smee turned to sharpen the razor on the strop, and an exhausted sea gull decided to settle onto the warm, cozy towel for a short nap. Smee, whose eyesight was quite poor, started to lather the bird's rump.

"You know, Captain," said Smee as he began to shave the sea gull's behind, "I can't help noticing that you ain't been your usual jolly self of late. And the crew's getting a might uneasy, too. That is, what's left of the crew."

Smee put down the razor and patted some aftershave on the sea gull's bare bottom. He turned away for a moment. The sea gull awoke with a start and flew off squawking.

"Why don't we put to sea, Captain?" continued Smee conversationally. He poured some powder into his hands. "We'd all be a lot happier and a lot healthier if we left Never Land and forgot about Peter Pan.

"Oh dear," mumbled Smee suddenly, feeling about in the towel. "I never shaved him this close before."

Smee searched the deck, thinking he had cut off the captain's head. "Don't worry, Captain," he promised nervously, crawling around and under everything on deck. "It must be around here somewhere."

Smee was under the captain's chair when the towel slid from Hook's face.

"Get up, you idiot!" the captain shouted impatiently.

Smee jumped, knocking the chair *and* Hook into a tumble.

"Why, you blithering blockhead!" Hook jumped to his feet and caught Smee by the shirt. He might have made the mate walk the plank had it not been for a call from the crow's nest: "Peter Pan ahoy!"

"What!" Hook gasped. "Where?"

"Three points off the starboard bow!" shouted the lookout.

Hook grabbed a telescope and scanned the skies until he found Peter, Wendy, and her brothers flying toward Never Land. "Swoggle me eyes! It's Pan, and he's headed this way with some more of those scurvy brats! Mr. Smee! Pipe up the crew!"

"Aye, aye, Captain." Smee blew his whistle. "All hands on deck! All hands on deck!"

The pirate crew, armed with swords, daggers, and muskets, quickly assembled on the deck.

"We've got him this time, Mr. Smee," cried Hook gleefully. "I've waited years for this!"

"And that's not counting the holidays, either," Smee reminded him.

"Man the Long Tom, you bilge rats!" Hook shouted at the sailors. "Double the powder and shorten the fuse."

Michael and John do battle as the imaginary characters
Peter Pan and Captain Hook.

Peter Pan arrives one night and proves he's real.

Peter shows the children how easy it is to fly.

Peter and the children fly away to Never Land... where children never grow up.

Peter takes Wendy to visit the Mermaid Lagoon.

John and Michael explore the island with the Lost Boys.

Peter infuriates Hook by dancing on his sword.

Captain Hook seeks his revenge by tricking Tinker Bell into revealing the location of Peter's secret hideout.

Hook and his men plan to capture the children outside the hideout.

Tinker Bell warns Peter that the ticking gift is a bomb from Captain Hook!

On the pirate ship, Wendy is forced to walk the plank.

Peter saves Wendy just in the nick of time.

John leads the Lost Boys in battle against the pirates.

Peter defeats Captain Hook once and for all.

Back home, Wendy and her parents gaze at a strange cloud in the sky.

The cloud looks just like...Captain Hook's pirate ship!

Hook turned the telescope to the sky and found his prey again. Peter, Wendy, and the boys were perched on a cloud.

"Ah, a pretty sight," Hook said with a wicked smile. "We'll pot 'em like sitting ducks. All right men, range forty-two!"

The pirates on deck saluted "Aye, aye" and adjusted the cannon.

"Elevation sixty-five," said Hook. "Three degrees west. Steady now, steady!"

Meanwhile, on the cloud above, Peter and the Darling children gazed down on the magnificent island of Never Land.

"Oh, Peter," Wendy said happily. "It's just as I've always dreamed it would be. Look, John, there's Mermaid Lagoon!"

"By Jove!" said John, pointing with his umbrella. "And there's the Indian camp!"

Not to be outdone, Michael found something familiar of his own. "Look, there's Captain Hook and the pirates!"

No sooner had the words left his lips than there was a terrific BOOM! followed by a large puff of smoke. A huge cannonball was hurtling straight toward them!

4

The cannonball whizzed harmlessly past as the Darling children jumped behind a cloud.

"Quick, Tink!" said Peter. "Take Wendy and the boys to the island. I'll stay here and draw Hook's fire."

Tinker Bell dashed like a tiny shooting star downward to the island. It was all Wendy, John, and Michael could do to keep up. Meanwhile, Peter stood on the cloud and waved down to the ship.

"Hook, you old codfish!" he taunted. "Here! Up here!"

Hook answered by sending up two more cannonballs. With merry nonchalance, Peter danced out of their path.

Wendy was having a more difficult time. "Tinker Bell!" Wendy cried. "Not so fast! Please, Tinker Bell, we can't keep up with you. Wait!"

Tinker Bell seemed not to hear Wendy's pleadings. Leaving Wendy and the boys far behind, Tinker Bell shot down into the forest in a trail of fairy dust and disappeared through a trapdoor in Hangman's Tree. She raced through the dark underground grotto that led to Peter's secret hideaway. There she found the Lost Boys asleep in their animal costumes.

Tinker Bell tried to rouse Skunk and Rabbit. Finally, she managed to push a wooden club onto Foxy's head.

"Ouch!" Foxy cried out, rubbing his sore head. Thinking Cubby was the culprit, he kicked him so hard that the boy rolled over and knocked into the Raccoon Twins. Now the Raccoon Twins wanted to fight, and Cubby, the biggest of the boys, was only too happy to oblige. Soon the boys, including Skunk, were tangled up in the ruckus, punching and kicking and hitting. Tinker Bell flew among them, desperately trying to get their attention. Finally, she pulled Foxy's hair until he stopped fighting and looked up. Tinker Bell jingled.

"Orders from Pan?" Foxy gasped. He yelled at the boys to stop.

"What are the orders, Tink?" Rabbit asked.

Tinker Bell jingled and danced an elaborate pantomime.

"A terrible what?" asked Cubby. Tinker Bell flapped her arms.

"A Wendy bird," Foxy said. "Flying this way."

Tinker Bell kept jingling. "Pan's orders are to smash it?" Cubby asked.

"Kick it?" Foxy guessed.

Tinker Bell pretended to take aim along the barrel of an imaginary gun.

"Shoot it down!" Foxy cried.

"Yes!" chorused the others. "Shoot it down!"

There was a mad scramble for slingshots and peashooters as the Lost Boys tumbled after Tinker Bell. Outside the hideout, Tinker Bell landed on the branch of a tree and pointed upward.

"I see it!" said Foxy. The Lost Boys took aim with their rocks and sticks and slingshots.

"Ready, aim, fire!"

Rather perturbed that Tinker Bell had flown off so hastily, a confused Wendy suddenly found herself frantically dodging a mad volley of flying sticks and stones. With no time to think wonderful thoughts, she began to fall.

From her perch, Tinker Bell smiled and clapped her tiny hands as Wendy plummeted toward the jagged rocks.

At the last second, however, Peter swooped in and caught her.

36

"Oh, Peter, you saved me!" cried Wendy with delight, and she hugged him. Tinker Bell was so furious that she turned as red as hot metal and flew right through a leaf, leaving a smoldering hole behind.

Michael and John floated down to join their sister and Peter. A moment later the Lost Boys burst through the foliage, waving their weapons and shouting gleefully, "Pan! Hey, Pan! We followed your orders."

"I got it with my skull buster," said Foxy proudly.

"No you didn't!" shouted the Raccoon Twins. "We got it."

"No, I did it, Pan," Rabbit insisted. "It was me!"

A tussle broke out among the Lost Boys over who had actually felled the Wendy bird.

"Attention!" Peter shouted. The Lost Boys quickly fell silent. Peter put his hands on his hips. "I'm certainly proud of you . . . *block-heads!*"

The Lost Boys were confused. They had expected Peter to be pleased with them. Instead he was angry.

"I bring you a mother to tell you stories," Peter scolded them, "and you shoot her down."

37

"Tink said it was a bird," Cubby sniffed.

"She said you said to shoot it down," explained Rabbit.

On a branch in a nearby tree, Peter spied Tinker Bell tiptoeing away.

"Tinker Bell," Peter said crossly. "Come here."

She stopped and turned toward Peter. "You are charged with high treason, Tink," he said. "Are you guilty or not?"

Tinker Bell yawned and turned away. "Guilty?" Peter asked. "But Tink," he called out, "don't you know you might have killed her?"

Tinker Bell peeped out from behind a leaf and nodded.

"Tinker Bell," Peter commanded, "I hereby banish you forever!"

Tinker Bell stamped her feet angrily.

But Wendy had a forgiving nature. "Peter, please," she begged. "Not forever."

Peter reconsidered. "Well, all right, for a week then." But it was already too late. Tinker Bell had flown far away and could not hear him. In any case Peter's thoughts quickly skipped to a new topic. "Come on, Wendy, I'll show you the island."

"The mermaids?" Wendy asked excitedly.

Peter agreed. But Cubby wasn't so sure he wanted to visit the mermaids. "Let's go hunting," he suggested.

"Tigers?" Rabbit asked.

"No," said the Raccoon Twins. "Bears."

"Personally," said John, "I should prefer to see the aborigines."

"And the Indians, too," said Michael.

"All right, men," Peter said. "Go out and explore the island."

The boys saluted. Peter pointed at John. "You be the leader."

"I shall try to be worthy of my post," replied John with humility. Then he gestured grandly toward the jungle with his umbrella and ordered the Lost Boys to march. Michael trailed behind, dragging his teddy bear.

"Do be careful," Wendy called after them.

John followed a trail that took them through jungles and fields and forests. They crossed tree bridges and rivers, swung on vines, and hopped over rocks. Finally, in a forest clearing, John stopped to study a footprint in the soft earth.

"The Blackfoot tribe," he said importantly. "Part of the Algonquin group. Quite a formidable opponent, I must say."

"Let's go get 'em!" Cubby shouted. The boys scrambled in all directions.

"Gentlemen, please!" said John, holding up his umbrella in an attempt to control his troops. "First, we must plan our strategy."

"What's *strategy?*" asked a bewildered Cubby.

"Our plan of attack," John explained patiently. With the tip of his umbrella, he drew a circle around the footprint. "The initial phase is an encircling maneuver."

As John explained his strategy to the Lost Boys, Michael was wandering through the woods toward the clearing. He'd fallen behind the others and was just now catching up. On the path he spied a red-and-white feather on the ground and bent down to pick it up. "Now I'm an Indian," said Michael as he put the feather in his hair.

Then he noticed something strange. A small tree seemed to be following him. No matter how far he walked, the tree was always the same distance behind.

Curious, Michael went back to the tree and lifted its branches. Underneath was a pair of moccasins. Michael let go of the branch and ran.

"Indians!" Michael cried as he came

upon John and the Lost Boys. "John! Indians!"

But the older boys were too engrossed in designing their strategy to notice Michael. "The Indians are cunning," John was saying, "but so are we. Therefore, we surround them and take them by surprise."

Suddenly half a dozen small trees pounced on them as the Indians launched their own surprise attack. Before long the boys found themselves being dragged to the Indian camp, where they were tied to a totem pole and surrounded by Indians beating tom-toms. John felt positively mortified that he'd led the boys into this mess.

"I'm frightfully sorry, old chaps," John apologized. "It's all my fault."

"Aw, that's all right," said Cubby.

"We don't mind," added Foxy.

Then John looked up into the painted face of the big Indian chief, who was wearing a grand feather headdress with pointed buffalo horns sticking out on either side.

"Welcome," the chief grunted in greeting.

"Hiya, Chief," said Cubby.

"Greetings," said John and Michael.

The chief sketched his hands in the air. "For many moons," he said, "we have fought the Lost Boys. Sometimes you win, sometimes we win."

"That's right, Chief," said Cubby, nodding. "This time you win. Now let us go."

John blinked, "Let us go?" he asked, puzzled. "You mean this is only a game?"

"Sure," said Foxy. "When we win, we turn them loose."

"And when they win, they turn us loose," said one of the Raccoon Twins.

The chief shook his head. "This time we are not going to turn anyone loose."

"The chief's a big spoofer." Foxy laughed.

"This is no spoof," the chief explained with great seriousness. "Where are you hiding Princess Tiger Lily?"

"Tiger Lily?" Cubby repeated in surprise.

"We ain't got your princess," said Foxy.

"I've certainly never seen her," John said.

"Us, neither," said the others.

"That is a big lie!" The chief glowered. "If Tiger Lily is not back by sunset, you will all burn at the stake."

The Lost Boys gasped. It wasn't a game anymore.

5

O n the opposite side of the island, Peter
and Wendy sat on a cliff overlooking
a beautiful blue lagoon. Below them
half a dozen mermaids played in the water or
lounged lazily on rocks below a waterfall.

"Just imagine," Wendy mused out loud.
"Real live mermaids."

"Want to meet them?" Peter asked.

"Oh, Peter, I'd love to," Wendy said.

"Then come on." Peter jumped off the
rock and hopped easily down the steep face of
the cliff. Wendy was left to climb among the
rocks on her own. She got as far as the last
rock, then decided she might need help.

"Oh, Peter," she called. "Peter!"

The mermaids turned and looked dis-
dainfully at Wendy.

"What's *she* doing here?" one of them
asked Peter huffily.

"And in her nightdress, too," said another
disapprovingly.

The mermaids swam over to where
Wendy was balanced rather precariously on a

small rock surrounded by water.

"Come, dearie," taunted one. "Join us for a swim!" She reached to pull Wendy into the water.

"But I'm not dressed," Wendy demurred.

"But you must! We insist!"

Wendy fended off the mermaids as best she could. They began to splash her with their tails, so, losing patience, Wendy angrily picked up a seashell and threatened to throw it. Peter flew up and snatched the shell out of Wendy's hands.

"They were just having some fun," he said, turning to the mermaids. "Weren't you, girls?"

One of the mermaids nodded innocently. "We were only trying to drown her."

Wendy knew they'd been serious. "If you think that I'm going to put up with—"

Peter clamped his hand over her mouth. "Shhh," he whispered. "Hold it." A ticking sound could be heard not far off. Peter flew to a small rock at the mouth of the lagoon to investigate. "It's Captain Hook!"

"Hook!" cried the mermaids. They dove to safety in the water. Peter led Wendy to the rock and pointed. Hook was standing in the bow of a rowboat, and Smee was rowing. In the stern sat a beautiful Indian princess, her hands tied behind her back with rope. The crocodile trailed after the rowboat like a shadow. Ticktock. Ticktock.

"They've captured Tiger Lily," Peter whispered to Wendy. "Looks like they're heading for Skull Rock. Come on, let's see what they're up to."

Peter took Wendy by the hand, and they flew to a huge, hollow rock in the shape of a skull. Inside Skull Rock they perched on a ledge high above the pool where Hook and Smee were steering their boat. Wendy and Peter watched as Smee forced Tiger Lily onto a small rock surrounded by water. He then tied a heavy anchor to the rope at her ankles.

"Now, my dear princess," Hook said, "this is my proposition. You tell me the hiding place of Peter Pan and I shall set you free."

Tiger Lily refused to speak.

Hook leaned closer. "You'd better talk, my dear. Soon the tide will be in, and then it will be too late. Remember, there's no path to the happy hunting ground through water."

Peter had to save Tiger Lily. He hid himself behind a rock outside the entrance to Skull Rock and called out in a deep, rumbling voice, "Manatoa, great spirit of mighty seawater, speak. Beware, Captain Hook, beware!"

"Did you hear that, Smee?" asked a startled Captain Hook.

Smee was trembling like a leaf. "It's an evil spirit," he said.

Hook was suspicious. He drew out his long sword. "Stay here while I have a look around," he told Smee.

Hook climbed gingerly toward the outer rocks to find this so-called spirit. Meanwhile, Peter slipped back inside Skull Rock and cupped his hat against his mouth.

"Mr. Smee!" he intoned in the voice of Captain Hook.

"Yes? Yes?" replied the surprised mate.

"Release the princess and take her back to her people."

"But Captain!" muttered Smee.

"Those are my orders!" echoed the stern voice of Captain Hook.

Smee did as he was told and untied Tiger Lily. "Well, at least the captain's come to his senses," he mumbled to himself. "I told him all along the Indians wouldn't betray Peter Pan."

Outside the cave, Hook was astounded to find Smee calmly rowing back to the ship with Tiger Lily.

"And just what do you think you're doing?" he inquired blandly.

"Carrying out your orders," answered a bewildered Smee.

"My orders?" repeated Hook. He gave the boat an angry kick. "Put her back, you blithering idiot."

Smee obliged and rowed back into Skull Rock, mumbling all the while. But no sooner had Smee tied up Tiger Lily for the second time than *again* came the captain's voice. "Just what do you think you're doing?"

"Putting her back just as you said," said Smee witheringly.

"I said nothing of the sort!" roared the imposter Hook. "Take the princess back to her people!"

Smee wasn't the only person who had heard the angry words. Hook had heard them as well and instantly realized what was happening. It's that blasted Pan, Hook told himself, trying to make a fool of me again. Hook began to climb quietly toward the voice.

Meanwhile, Peter was having a great deal of fun at Smee's expense. "And one more thing," he shouted in Hook's voice. "When you return to the ship, tell the whole crew to help themselves to my best rum!"

Little did Peter know that the pirate captain had sneaked up behind him, his silver hook raised high, ready to strike. Luckily, Wendy caught sight of him.

"Peter!" cried Wendy as Hook climbed out above the ledge.

Peter ducked as the hook swung down, pinning his hat to the rock.

"Scurvy brat!" Hook swore as Peter darted up and down and around. Hook brandished his long sword and shouted, "Come down, boy, if you've a taste for cold steel."

Not one to shirk a challenge, Peter found himself locked in a duel with the pirate captain on a thin cliff high above the water. Back and forth they went, Hook slashing with his sword, Peter defending with his dagger.

"Give it to him, Captain!" yelled Smee. "Cleave him to the brisket!"

Knife and sword blades clanged loudly as the duel raged on. Hook lunged repeatedly, but Peter skipped back and parried. Suddenly Hook batted Peter's dagger from his hand.

"I've got you this time, Pan," Hook shouted with glee. Peter smiled. Hook had inadvertently stepped off the ledge into midair and only just now realized it.

"Ahhh!" Hook screamed as he managed

to catch hold of the rock with his hook.

"Well, well," Peter chuckled, alighting on the rocks above. "A codfish on a hook."

"I'll get you for this!" Hook swore. "If it's the last thing I do."

"I say, Captain," Peter said, cupping a hand to his ear. "Do you hear something?"

Hook's eyes went wide with fright. "No!" he cried as the ticking sound grew louder. "Noooo!"

Far below, the crocodile raised his head from the water and licked his hungry jaws.

"Oh, Mr. Crocodile?" Peter sang out and waved. "Do you like codfish?"

The crocodile leapt up and snapped at Hook's coattail. Rippp! The coat tore away. The crocodile leapt again and snagged Hook's pants. Hook clung desperately to the cliff, but the rock began to crumble. Suddenly it gave way. Hook let out a scream, fell, and was swallowed up in the crocodile's mouth. An instant later the crocodile disappeared under the water.

Wendy let out a horrified gasp.

Suddenly the crocodile burst out of the water. Hook had the crocodile's jaws forced wide apart.

"*Smeeeeeeee!*" cried Hook.

Smee dashed for the rowboat as the crocodile's jaws snapped shut. Hook cried out and dove into the water. The crocodile snapped and snapped. *"Smeeeeeeee!"* Round and round swam the captain, with the crocodile in eager pursuit.

Peter stood at the edge of Skull Rock and crowed in triumph as he watched Captain Hook swimming for all he was worth out to sea. Wendy tapped him on the shoulder. "What about Tiger Lily?"

Peter had forgotten about her! In a flash he shot back inside Skull Rock. Already the tide had risen above her head—another second and she would have drowned. Peter plunged into the water and lifted her to safety. With Tiger Lily in his arms, he and Wendy flew out of Skull Rock and toward the Indian camp.

6

Hook had a terrible cold and a splitting headache. Once again Peter Pan had managed to make a fool of him. "Curse that Peter Pan!" Hook muttered to himself for the hundredth time.

It was something Smee had mentioned almost casually that lifted his spirits and convinced Hook that this time—finally—he would have Peter Pan.

"Did you say Peter has banished Tinker Bell?" Hook asked.

"Aye, Captain," Smee answered. "That he has."

The news was incredible. Hook was taken aback. "But why?" he demanded.

"Well," Smee explained, "on account of Wendy, Captain. Tink tried to do her in, she did!" Hook could not believe his ears. "Tink is terrible jealous," Smee said.

"Well, well," said the captain as he stroked his chin with his hook. A plan was beginning to take shape in his head.

"That's it!" he cried suddenly.

Smee smiled agreeably.

"Smee," said Hook with a delicious gleam in his eye, "get me my best dress coat!"

Smee went for the coat, and Hook refined his plan. If he could convince Tinker Bell that he wanted to help get rid of Wendy, she might just lead him to Peter Pan's hiding place. Smee returned with the captain's best coat and gold hook, then started to leave.

"Where do you think you're going?" Smee shrugged uncertainly. Hook collared him. "You're going ashore to pick up Tinker Bell and bring her to me. Understand?"

"Aye, aye, Captain," Smee saluted.

Meanwhile, the chief had been so relieved by the safe return of Tiger Lily that he made Peter an honorary chief, Little Flying Eagle, and ordered a big celebration. Michael, John, and the Lost Boys were all freed and made honorary braves, too, and each was given a feather to wear. Peter let out a whoop, and everyone cheered.

Soon they were all singing and dancing around the campfire, having a wonderful time. A large Indian woman with a papoose on her back stepped up to Wendy.

"Stop dancing," she ordered. "Get firewood."

Get firewood. But Wendy wanted to dance and shout like her brothers and Peter. The Indian woman pointed toward the woods. Oh well, Wendy shrugged. She wished not to offend the Indians, and if collecting some firewood would make them happy, she'd do it. But when Wendy returned to camp with an armload of wood, she saw Tiger Lily dancing and shouting and having a wonderful time. What was worse, she was rubbing noses with Peter!

Wendy fumed and threw down the wood. Just then John, Michael, and the Lost Boys danced past her. Michael handed her his teddy bear.

"Take the papoose," he commanded grandly.

Wendy was shocked. Since when did she take orders from her baby brother? And to make matters worse, the Indian woman returned.

"Get firewood," she ordered again.

Wendy stomped her foot defiantly. "I won't get firewood!" she corrected. "I'm going home!" She marched out of the Indian camp and into the dark.

Not far away, Tinker Bell listened sadly to the celebrating. She was heartbroken. First, Peter had brought that awful Wendy to Never

Land, and now he was dancing with Tiger Lily. It wasn't fair, she told herself. Tinker Bell sighed. She didn't notice that Mr. Smee had sneaked up behind her. Smee quickly snatched Tinker Bell up in his cap.

"Begging your pardon, Miss Bell," Smee chuckled as he twisted the cap shut, "but Captain Hook would like a word with you."

A short time later Tinker Bell found herself in Captain Hook's cabin aboard the pirate ship. Hook played piano and Smee drank wine from a keg while Tinker Bell sat on a corked bottle and tried to ignore them both.

"I admit defeat, Miss Bell," sighed Captain Hook ruefully. "Tomorrow I'll leave this island and never return. That's why I asked you over, my dear. To tell Peter I bear him no ill will."

Tinker Bell gave Hook a suspicious look, turned her back to him, and crossed her arms. It was a look that seemed to suggest that she hardly cared whether Hook bore ill will or not.

"Pan does have his faults," Hook continued. "For instance, bringing *that Wendy* to the island." He gave Tinker Bell a quick, meaningful glance. "Rumor has it," he added significantly, "that she's already come between you and Peter."

Tinker Bell sniffed. How she wished that awful Wendy had never come to Never Land. Just the thought of her with Peter made Tinker Bell start to cry.

"Think of it, Smee," Hook said with an elaborate show of fake sympathy. "A man takes the best years of a maid's life . . . and then casts her aside like an old glove."

Tinker Bell nodded in agreement at the injustice of it all. That was exactly what Peter had done. Her tears turned to sobs.

Even Smee's eyes were wet. "Ain't it a bloomin' shame?"

Hook nodded sadly and graciously offered Tinker Bell a handkerchief. "Now, we mustn't judge Peter too harshly. It's really Wendy who's to blame."

Tinker Bell dried her eyes. Hook was right, she told herself. Everything *had been* fine until Wendy arrived. If only Peter hadn't gone back to the nursery for his shadow!

"I've got it, Smee!" said Hook suddenly. "We'll save the lad from himself!"

"But how?" Smee asked. "We sail in the morning."

"That's it!" Hook cried out as if suddenly overtaken with a brilliant idea. "We'll kidnap Wendy. Take her to sea with us. Once she's

gone, Peter will forget this mad infatuation."
He made for the door.

"Come, Smee," Hook shouted. "We must leave immediately and surround Peter's home."

"But Captain," objected Smee. "We don't know where Peter Pan lives."

Hook stopped in the doorway. "Great Scott!" he exclaimed, suddenly remembering. He looked back to Smee helplessly. "You're right!"

Tinker Bell eagerly flew to the map on the captain's table and jingled.

"What?" asked Hook, feigning innocence. "You could show us the way to Peter's hideout? Why, I never thought of that!" He came back to the table and watched as Tinker Bell slowly outlined the route. He grew impatient at one point. "Get on with it!" he snapped, then quickly caught himself.

Tinker Bell flew up and jingled scoldingly.

"Harm Peter?" said Hook innocently. "I give my word never to lay a finger—or a hook on him."

Satisfied, Tinker Bell revealed the location of Peter's hideaway on the map.

"Hangman's Tree!" Hook cried with delight. He

grabbed Tinker Bell and sneered. "Thank you, my dear, you've been most helpful." He thrust her into a lantern and locked its door.

With a start, Tinker Bell realized what she'd done. She'd betrayed Peter! Hook had never wanted Wendy. It was Peter he'd been after all along. She banged frantically against the glass, trying to escape. She had to warn Peter!

7

The boys danced all the way from the Indian camp to Hangman's Tree and then·slid down the secret entrance to the hideout. They danced past Wendy, who was sitting on the edge of her bed. She appeared thoroughly unamused.

"Big Chief Flying Eagle greets his braves," Peter crowed as he made his triumphant entrance. The boys dropped to their knees and bowed. "Big Chief greets Little Mother," Peter told Wendy.

"Ugh," said Wendy sourly as she turned away.

"Aw, Wendy." Peter's voice was etched with disappointment. "Is that all you have to say? Everyone else thinks I'm wonderful."

"Especially Tiger Lily," said Wendy sharply. "John, Michael," she said to the boys, "take off that war paint and get ready for bed."

"Bed?" said John.

"Braves don't sleep." Michael crossed his arms resolutely. "We go days without sleep."

"But we're going home in the morning," said Wendy.

"Home!" John gasped.

"We don't want to go home," Michael complained.

"Don't go home!" Peter said in a commanding tone. "Wendy and the boys will stay—and have a good time."

Wendy felt her patience being tested.

"Now Peter," Wendy said. "Let's stop pretending and be practical."

But Peter had no interest in being practical. "Chief Flying Eagle has spoken," he said pompously. He crossed his arms and stalked into his own room. The boys broke out into a raucous cheer.

"Oh, for goodness' sake, boys." Wendy tried to calm John and Michael down. "Do you want to stay here and grow up like . . . like Peter and the Lost Boys?"

"Yes!" Michael cried.

"But you can't," insisted Wendy, buttoning up his pink pajamas. "You need a mother."

"Aren't you our mother?" Michael asked.

"Of course not," Wendy replied. "Surely you haven't forgotten our real mother."

"Did she have silky ears and wear a fur coat?" Michael asked.

"No, Michael, that was Nana," Wendy said.

Across the room, the Lost Boys stopped playing and listened.

"I think I had a mother once," Cubby said.

"What was she like?" asked one of the Raccoon Twins.

"I forget," Cubby admitted.

"I had a white rat once," said Foxy.

"That's no mother!" Cubby said angrily.

As usual, when the Lost Boys disagreed about something, a loud ruckus ensued.

"Boys! Boys!" cried Wendy impatiently. "Please stop. I'll tell you what a mother is."

The Lost Boys stopped fighting and settled in a tight circle around Wendy. She sat down on the bed and took Michael onto her lap.

"Well," Wendy began, "a mother is the most wonderful person in the world. She's the angel voice that bids you good night, kisses your cheek, and whispers, 'Sleep tight.'"

The boys listened raptly. Those who remembered their mothers now missed them dearly. Those who couldn't remember wished they could. They slowly wiped the war paint from their faces and pulled the feathers from their headbands.

Michael put his arms around his big sister and sniffed. "I want to see my mother."

"I propose we leave for home at once!" John declared, grabbing his hat.

"Could I go, too?" Cubby asked.

"Us, too!" said the other Lost Boys. They begged Wendy to take them with her.

"All right, boys," she said. "I'm sure Mother would be glad to have you. That is, if Peter doesn't mind."

Peter stuck his head out from behind the curtain to his room. "Go ahead," he said grumpily. "Go back and grow up. But I'm warning you," he added severely. "Once you grow up, you can never come back. Never!"

He disappeared back into his room. The boys were surprised at the harshness of his words, but their thoughts soon turned again to having a mother.

"Shall we be off, men?" called John, who was standing near the exit. The boys lined up and started out. Wendy paused as she passed by Peter's room.

"Peter?" she called hopefully. There was no answer. Wendy whispered a final sad farewell and left the tree house.

At the entrance to Hangman's Tree, Wendy gasped. Captain Hook and his band of pirates had captured the boys! A rough hand then came down over her mouth.

"Take them away, men," Hook ordered. The pirates led the children back to the ship. Hook and Smee gazed down into the secret entrance.

"And now, Smee," said Hook, "we'll take care of Master Peter Pan." He lowered a box tied with a ribbon into Peter's lair.

"Wouldn't it be more humanelike to slit his throat?" Smee asked.

"Aye, it would." Hook sniggered. "But I gave my word not to lay a finger—or a hook— on Peter Pan. And Captain Hook never breaks a promise."

Having left the mysterious box where Peter was sure to find it, Hook and Smee quickly made their way back to the ship.

8

O n board the pirate ship, Wendy and the boys found themselves tied to the mast. At the far end of the deck, Hook sat at a table with his pirate log open before him. He dangled a quill pen over the book.

"Sign on as a pirate today and you'll get a free tattoo," he told the boys. "But I'll be frank. If you don't sign up, you'll walk the plank!"

Hook dipped the quill in a pot of ink. "Free the boys," he ordered.

A pirate near the mast cut the rope. The boys ran, anxious to sign.

"Boys!" cried Wendy disapprovingly. "Aren't you ashamed of yourselves?"

The boys skidded to a halt.

"But Captain Hook is most insistent," John tried to explain.

"Yeah," said Cubby. "If we don't sign up, he said we'll walk the plank."

"No, we won't." Wendy defiantly turned her nose up at Hook. "Peter Pan will save us."

Hook and Smee laughed heartily.

"A thousand pardons, my dear," Hook said once he'd caught his breath. "But I don't believe you're in on our little joke. You see, we left a present for Peter. A sort of surprise, you might say. Why, I can see our little friend at this very moment reading the tender inscription."

"It says," Smee giggled, "'To Peter, with love, from Wendy. Do not open until six o'clock.'"

"If Peter could see within the package, he'd find an ingenious little device inside," Hook explained. "A bomb set so that when the clock strikes six, Peter will be blasted out of Never Land forever!"

"Oh no!" Wendy gasped.

She wasn't the only one dismayed by the news. Trapped inside the lantern in Hook's cabin, Tinker Bell overheard Hook's plan and saw from the cabin clock that the appointed hour was only minutes away. She rocked the lantern back and forth until it tipped over and broke open. In a flash Tinker Bell shot out the porthole and sped toward the island, leaving a trail of dust behind.

In his hideout, Peter had found the mysterious box and was waiting impatiently for the clock on the wall to strike six. He wondered what it could be. At twelve seconds to six, his curiosity got the best of him and he decided to open the box. But just as he started to undo the ribbon, Tinker Bell flew into the room, jingling frantically.

"Hi, Tink." Peter showed her the box. "Look what Wendy left."

Tinker Bell instantly tried to pull the box away.

"Hey, stop it!" Peter pulled the box back. "What's the matter with you?"

Tinker Bell jingled as fast as she could.

"A bomb?" said Peter skeptically. "Don't be ridiculous."

Inside the box, the clock attached to the bomb struck six. As the alarm began to ring, Tinker Bell dove toward Peter and whisked the box away.

From the deck of the pirate ship Wendy cried out as an enormous explosion rocked the island. The ship reeled sideways, and pieces of trees and rocks were hurtled hundreds of yards into the air.

Hook ceremoniously removed his hat and held it over his heart. "And so passeth a worthy opponent," he said solemnly.

Little did Hook suspect that Peter was still alive. Thanks to Tinker Bell he had been spared the full effect of the blast. Desperately he crawled out from under the rubble of rock and boulder that had once been his hideout.

"Tink?" Peter called out. "Tinker Bell?"

A faint tinkling sound came from somewhere under the rubble.

"Where are you?" Peter cried, digging frantically through the debris. "Are you all right?"

Tinker Bell jingled weakly. She was trying to tell him about Wendy and the boys aboard the pirate ship.

"But I have to save you first!" Peter clawed through the broken timbers. Loose debris showered down around him, nearly burying him, but he ducked out of the way and kept digging. Ahead through the broken tree limbs and past the overturned rocks, he could see Tinker Bell's faint glow. "Hold on, Tink! Hold on!"

But Tinker Bell's glow was fading.

"Don't go out!" Peter cried. "Don't you understand? You mean more to me than anything in the whole world."

The glow from Tinker Bell flared momentarily, then faded. Just as Peter reached her, a huge boulder gave way, and a torrent of rock and wood crashed down, leaving nothing but dust and silence.

9

Aboard the pirate ship, Hook once
again offered Wendy and the boys a
choice: "Which will it be? The pen . . .
or the plank?"

"We will never join your crew," Wendy
stated bravely.

"As you wish," replied Hook with a
malicious grin. He pointed to the plank.
"Ladies first, my dear."

Even at the end, Wendy remained stoic.
She turned to the Lost Boys and said good-
bye, then patted John on the head. "Be brave,
John."

"I shall strive to, Wendy." John stood tall
and puffed out his chest, but he was very sad.

Michael wiped a tear from his eye, and
Wendy gave him a farewell kiss on the cheek.
But before she could tell him how much she
loved him, she was grabbed by a large pirate.
"Go on with ya!" he growled.

Once again the boys were tied to the
mast, where they watched in dismay as the
pirates pushed Wendy toward the plank.

Wendy held her head high as she walked slowly onto the plank and out over the placid waters. On deck behind her, the bloodthirsty pirates shouted impatiently. Oh, Peter, Wendy thought, gazing up at the cloudy gray sky, if only you were here. She reached the end of the plank and hesitated. A tear rolled off her cheek and dropped into the salty water below. There was no turning back, Wendy told herself. She stepped off the plank and promptly disappeared.

On deck, Hook and others listened for the splash. They waited . . . and waited.

"Captain!" Smee gasped. "No splash!"

Mr. Smee was right—Wendy had made no splash. Not a sound. Hook and the others rushed to the railing and peered down into the still water.

"Not a bloomin' ripple," one of the pirates whispered. "It's a jinx!"

"The ship's bewitched!" another pirate cried.

Hook spun around and caught him by the shirt. "So you want a splash? I'll give you a splash." He angrily threw the offending pirate over the side, then turned to the rest of the crew. "Who's next?" he demanded.

"You're next, Hook," a voice shouted

from above. Startled, Hook looked up. Peter Pan and Wendy were in the crow's nest—and Tinker Bell, too! She was alive!

"This time you've gone too far, Hook!" Peter shook his fist.

"It's Pan and Wendy!" the boys cried.

"It can't be!" Hook was dumbfounded.

"It's his ghost!" Smee cried.

"Say your prayers, Hook." Peter drew his dagger and dove down toward the deck.

"I'll show you this ghost has blood in his veins!" Hook shouted as he drew his long sword.

A moment later Peter landed on the deck, and a ferocious duel ensued. Peter and Hook fought back and forth across the deck and around the mast. Hook at last lunged and took a mighty swing at Peter and missed, burying his hook deep in the mast.

"Curse it!" the captain snarled. While Hook tried to free himself from the wood, Peter cut the rope away from the boys.

"Come on, everybody!" he yelled. The boys started to climb the ship's rigging toward the crow's nest.

"Don't just stand there!" Hook screamed at his men. "Get those scurvy brats!"

Pirates with daggers clenched in their

teeth scrambled after the boys up the rigging. In the crow's nest, armed with rocks, sticks, and slingshots, the boys nervously readied themselves.

"Steady, men. Hold your fire," John warned them cautiously.

The pirates climbed higher.

"Steady." John's voice wavered.

Just as the lead pirate reached the crow's nest, John yelled, "Fire!"

The boys unleashed a barrage. One after another the pirates were beaten back until only the largest, most bloodthirsty pirate remained clinging to the bottom of the crow's nest, swinging his shining broad cutlass.

"Down, you blackguard!" John whacked him repeatedly on the head with his umbrella. Meanwhile, the other pirates had started up the rigging again. Tinker Bell saw that the boys were in trouble and raced down to tell Peter, who was still locked in a duel with Hook.

Peter deftly ducked under Hook's sword, then kicked him in the chin so hard that Hook tumbled backward and crashed into one of the ship's cannons. Peter flew up to the crow's nest. With a swish of his dagger, he cut the rigging and sent the pirates crashing down

71

into a small dinghy Smee had launched in an attempt to escape.

Hook finally regained his senses and cursed his men for abandoning ship. He was the only pirate left. Peter alighted on a yardarm. Hook looked up and shook his fist. "Fly, fly! You coward!"

"Coward?" answered Peter. "Me?"

"You wouldn't dare fight old Hook man to man," Captain Hook shouted as he climbed the rigging. "You'd fly away like a cowardly sparrow."

"Nobody calls me a coward and lives," Peter shouted back. "I'll fight you man to man with one hand tied behind my back!"

Hook pulled himself up onto the yardarm high above the ship's deck. He swung his sword forward, locking it against Peter's dagger.

"You won't fly?" he dared Peter.

"Don't do it, Peter!" Wendy cried from the crow's nest. "It's a trick."

But Peter wouldn't listen. "I give my word, Hook."

"Then let's have at it!" Hook cried. Before Peter knew what had happened, the pirate captain pushed him off the yardarm. Wendy and the boys gasped as Peter grabbed frantically for a rope to keep from plunging into the sea.

Hook's long sword slashed through the air, but Peter managed to pull himself back onto the yardarm. The duel continued across the spar. Several times Peter almost lost his balance as he tried to avoid Hook's blade.

Suddenly Hook batted the dagger out of Peter's hand. The pirate captain caught the knife and hurled it into the water below. "Insolent youth," the pirate captain snickered. "Prepare to die!"

"Fly!" Wendy cried from the crow's nest. "Please, Peter, fly!"

"No!" Peter shouted. "I gave my word."

As Hook pressed the sword forward, Peter inched back toward the end of the yardarm. His heart beat like a drum, and his throat felt tight and dry. As he looked around, he knew his choices were dismal: either fall into the sea and drown or be skewered by Hook's sword. Hook drew back his sword for one final thrust.

At the last second Peter noticed the black pirate flag fluttering over Hook's head. Catching Hook by surprise, he leapt up and pulled it down over the pirate captain's head. While Hook suddenly found himself tangled in the flag, Peter grabbed the sword away.

"You're mine, Hook," said Peter. Peter held the sword on the pirate captain. Still tangled in the flag, Hook stared out in disbelief while the boys shouted from the crow's nest: "Off with his head!" "Give him one, Peter!" "Cleave him to the brisket!"

"You wouldn't do old Hook in, now would you lad?" Hook begged as Peter kept the sword trained on him. "I'll go away forever. I'll do anything you say."

Peter considered the pirate's proposal. What was the worst, most despicable thing he could force Hook to do? Suddenly he knew. "All right," he said. "Say you're a codfish."

Hook swallowed and looked aghast.

"Say it!" Peter prodded him with the sword.

"I'm a . . . codfish," Hook whimpered.

"Louder!" Peter insisted.

"I'm a codfish!" Hook cried in disgrace. From the crow's nest came a cheer as the boys chanted, "Hook is a codfish! Hook is a codfish!"

"All right, Hook," Peter said, lowering the sword. "You're free to go . . . but you must never return."

Hook nodded meekly. Peter threw the sword into the sea and crowed in triumph.

"Look out, Peter!" Wendy cried.

The pirate swung his hook at Peter, but Peter ducked just in the nick of time. Hook lost his balance and began to teeter off the yardarm. A moment later he fell off the spar and plunged downward toward the sea . . . and into the waiting jaws of the crocodile!

The pirate captain disappeared down the great reptile's gullet. Was this finally the end of Hook? Peter and the others watched in amazement. Suddenly Hook burst out of the crocodile's mouth. He cried out for Smee and swam as fast as he could, zigzagging away into the sunset with the hungry crocodile nipping at his toes.

10

Wendy and the boys cheered.
"Hooray! Hooray for Captain Pan!"
Peter pulled on Hook's coat and
hat and playfully strutted across the poop
deck. "All right, ya swabs! Aloft with the sails!
We're casting off! Heave those halyards!"

Wendy looked at Peter and curtsied.
"But Peter . . . that is, Captain Pan."

"At your service, madam." Peter bowed
gallantly.

"Could you tell me, sir, where we're
sailing?"

Peter smiled and took the wheel. "To
London, of course."

Wendy clasped her hands with delight.
Her heart filled with joy. "Oh Peter!" she cried
happily, then turned to her brothers. "Michael,
John, we're going home!"

"Man the capstan!" Peter shouted as
they prepared to sail. "Hoist anchor! Pixie
dust!"

Tinker Bell danced up into the air and

sprinkled down pixie dust in a tinkling rain. Soon the entire ship had a golden glow, and it lifted off into the clouds under a full moon. Wendy hugged her brothers. Behind them Never Land grew smaller and smaller until it was just a memory.

In London, George and Mary Darling returned home from their party. George untied Nana and let the dog join them as they climbed the stairs to the nursery.

"I'm so glad you changed your mind about Wendy," Mary said as they climbed the stairs. "After all, she's still a child."

"Now, Mary, you know I never mean those things," George replied.

They reached the top of the stairs, and Mary pushed open the nursery door. The room was dark and quiet, but she was startled to find Wendy's bed empty. "Wendy?" she gasped.

Nana ran to the open window. Mary followed and found Wendy sleeping on the window seat. "Wendy, what on earth are you doing there?"

Wendy rubbed her sleepy eyes. When she saw her mother, she jumped up and ran into her arms. "Oh Mother! We're back!"

"Back?" asked her father.

"All except the Lost Boys," Wendy explained. "They weren't quite ready to grow up. That's why they went back to Never Land."

"Never Land?" George repeated.

"But *I* am," Wendy said.

"You're what?" asked her father.

"I'm ready to grow up," Wendy said proudly.

"Oh," he said.

Wendy hurried up to her mother, who was tucking the boys into their beds.

"Oh, Mother," said Wendy breathlessly. "It was such a wonderful adventure. Tinker Bell, and the mermaids, and Peter Pan. He was the most wonderful of all. Why, even when we were kidnapped, I knew—"

"Kidnapped?" George repeated with a gasp.

"Yes." Wendy nodded emphatically. "I knew Peter Pan would save us, and he did. And we all called Captain Hook a codfish, and then we sailed away on a ship into the sky."

"Mary," said George with a huge yawn, "I'm going to bed." He turned to leave the nursery.

Wendy returned to the window seat and gazed up at the sky. "Oh, Mother," she said dreamily, "he really is wonderful, isn't he? See how well he sails the ship?"

Mary smiled wistfully. She was just about to guide Wendy back to her bed when she looked up in the sky.

"George!" Mary shouted. "George!"

"Now what, Mary?" George asked irritably as he stopped at the doorway. But as he turned and looked back out the window, he suddenly caught his breath. Up in the sky, passing right in front of the full moon, was the most remarkable cloud he'd ever seen! It was shaped almost exactly like a sailing ship. George stepped closer to the window and felt goose bumps run up and down his arms.

"My word," he said with astonishment. "I have the strangest feeling that I've seen that ship before. A long time ago, when I was very young."

"Oh, George, dear," Mary whispered happily.

Wendy smiled, and together they watched the ship as it sailed past the moon on its journey home . . . to Never Land.